MAD LIBS®

UNDEAD
MAD LIBS

concept created by Roger Price & Leonard Stern

PSS!
PRICE STERN SLOAN
An Imprint of Penguin Group (USA) Inc.

PRICE STERN SLOAN
Published by the Penguin Group
Penguin Group (USA) Inc., 375 Hudson Street, New York, New York 10014, USA
Penguin Group (Canada), 90 Eglinton Avenue East, Suite 700,
Toronto, Ontario M4P 2Y3, Canada
(a division of Pearson Penguin Canada Inc.)
Penguin Books Ltd., 80 Strand, London WC2R 0RL, England
Penguin Group Ireland, 25 St. Stephen's Green, Dublin 2, Ireland
(a division of Penguin Books Ltd.)
Penguin Group (Australia), 250 Camberwell Road, Camberwell, Victoria 3124, Australia
(a division of Pearson Australia Group Pty. Ltd.)
Penguin Books India Pvt. Ltd., 11 Community Centre,
Panchsheel Park, New Delhi—110 017, India
Penguin Group (NZ), 67 Apollo Drive, Rosedale, Auckland 0632, New Zealand
(a division of Pearson New Zealand Ltd.)
Penguin Books (South Africa) (Pty.) Ltd., 24 Sturdee Avenue,
Rosebank, Johannesburg 2196, South Africa

Penguin Books Ltd., Registered Offices:
80 Strand, London WC2R 0RL, England

Published by Price Stern Sloan,
a division of Penguin Young Readers Group,
345 Hudson Street, New York, New York 10014.

ISBN 978-0-8431-9863-8

7   9   10   8

INSTRUCTIONS

MAD LIBS® is a game for people who don't like games!
It can be played by one, two, three, four, or forty.

• RIDICULOUSLY SIMPLE DIRECTIONS

In this tablet you will find stories containing blank spaces where words
are left out. One player, the READER, selects one of these stories. The
READER does not tell anyone what the story is about. Instead, he/she asks
the other players, the WRITERS, to give him/her words. These words are
used to fill in the blank spaces in the story.

• TO PLAY

The READER asks each WRITER in turn to call out a word—an adjective or
a noun or whatever the space calls for—and uses them to fill in the blank
spaces in the story. The result is a MAD LIBS® game.

When the READER then reads the completed MAD LIBS® game to the other
players, they will discover that they have written a story that is fantastic,
screamingly funny, shocking, silly, crazy, or just plain dumb—depending
upon which words each WRITER called out.

• EXAMPLE (*Before* and *After*)

"_____!" he said _____
    EXCLAMATION   ADVERB

as he jumped into his convertible _____ and
                NOUN

drove off with his _____ wife.
        ADJECTIVE

"_____*Ouch*_____!" he said _____*Stupidly*_____
    EXCLAMATION   ADVERB

as he jumped into his convertible _____*cat*_____ and
                NOUN

drove off with his _____*brave*_____ wife.
        ADJECTIVE

In case you have forgotten what adjectives, adverbs, nouns, and verbs are, here is a quick review:

An ADJECTIVE describes something or somebody. *Lumpy*, *soft*, *ugly*, *messy*, and *short* are adjectives.

An ADVERB tells how something is done. It modifies a verb and usually ends in "ly." *Modestly*, *stupidly*, *greedily*, and *carefully* are adverbs.

A NOUN is the name of a person, place, or thing. *Sidewalk*, *umbrella*, *bridle*, *bathtub*, and *nose* are nouns.

A VERB is an action word. *Run*, *pitch*, *jump*, and *swim* are verbs. Put the verbs in past tense if the directions say PAST TENSE. *Ran*, *pitched*, *jumped*, and *swam* are verbs in the past tense.

When we ask for A PLACE, we mean any sort of place: a country or city (*Spain*, *Cleveland*) or a room (*bathroom*, *kitchen*).

An EXCLAMATION or SILLY WORD is any sort of funny sound, gasp, grunt, or outcry, like *Wow!*, *Ouch!*, *Whomp!*, *Ick!*, and *Gadzooks!*

When we ask for specific words, like a NUMBER, a COLOR, an ANIMAL, or a PART OF THE BODY, we mean a word that is one of those things, like *seven*, *blue*, *horse*, or *head*.

When we ask for a PLURAL, it means more than one. For example, *cat* pluralized is *cats*.

MAD LIBS® is fun to play with friends, but you can also play it by yourself! To begin with, DO NOT look at the story on the page below. Fill in the blanks on this page with the words called for. Then, using the words you have selected, fill in the blank spaces in the story.

Now you've created your own hilarious MAD LIBS® game!

CONFESSIONS OF A VAMPIRE'S GIRLFRIEND

PART OF THE BODY (PLURAL) _____

PERSON IN ROOM (MALE) _____

ADJECTIVE _____

NOUN _____

ADJECTIVE _____

ADJECTIVE _____

PLURAL NOUN _____

PART OF THE BODY _____

ADJECTIVE _____

PART OF THE BODY (PLURAL) _____

NOUN _____

NUMBER _____

ADJECTIVE _____

MAD LIBS
CONFESSIONS OF A
VAMPIRE'S GIRLFRIEND

The moment I set my _____ on
<small>PART OF THE BODY (PLURAL)</small>

_____, I knew we were meant to be. He was
<small>PERSON IN ROOM (MALE)</small>

everything I wanted: tall, dark, and _____. But love at
<small>ADJECTIVE</small>

first _____ isn't always picture-_____.
<small>NOUN</small> <small>ADJECTIVE</small>

The first time he gave me a/an _____ rose, one of
<small>ADJECTIVE</small>

its _____ pricked my _____ and drew
<small>PLURAL NOUN</small> <small>PART OF THE BODY</small>

blood. While I tried to find a bandage for the wound, he followed

me to the bathroom—only to let loose a/an _____
<small>ADJECTIVE</small>

hiss, revealing his sharp _____. Luckily, he was
<small>PART OF THE BODY (PLURAL)</small>

able to restrain himself. But that's when I realized this hunky

_____ wasn't your average teenager. I had fallen in
<small>NOUN</small>

love with a/an _____-year-old vampire, and I was
<small>NUMBER</small>

_____ to be alive.
<small>ADJECTIVE</small>

MAD LIBS® is fun to play with friends, but you can also play it by yourself! To begin with, DO NOT look at the story on the page below. Fill in the blanks on this page with the words called for. Then, using the words you have selected, fill in the blank spaces in the story.

Now you've created your own hilarious MAD LIBS® game!

IN THE DEAD OF NIGHT

ADJECTIVE _____

NOUN _____

PERSON IN ROOM (FEMALE) _____

ADJECTIVE _____

ADJECTIVE _____

ADJECTIVE _____

NOUN _____

ADJECTIVE _____

ADVERB _____

ADJECTIVE _____

PART OF THE BODY _____

ADJECTIVE _____

PART OF THE BODY (PLURAL) _____

IN THE DEAD OF NIGHT

It was a/an _____ and stormy _____.
ADJECTIVE   NOUN

_____ was alone in the woods, shivering in
PERSON IN ROOM (FEMALE)

her _____ dress, trying to find her way home.
ADJECTIVE

Suddenly she tripped over something _____ on
ADJECTIVE

the ground. She took a closer look and discovered it was a/an

_____ tombstone! She was obviously in the middle of
ADJECTIVE

a/an _____-yard. Overcome by fear and struggling to
NOUN

stand up, she heard a/an _____ noise behind her. Someone
ADJECTIVE

or something was moving _____ toward her. She spun
ADVERB

around to get a better look and saw a/an _____ shadow
ADJECTIVE

moving past her. As the foggy figure came closer, she felt a cold

_____ touch her arm. Shaking free, she ran out of the
PART OF THE BODY

_____ cemetery as fast as her _____
ADJECTIVE   PART OF THE BODY (PLURAL)

could take her, never once looking back.

From UNDEAD MAD LIBS® · Copyright © 2011 by Price Stern Sloan,
an imprint of Penguin Group (USA) Inc., 345 Hudson Street, New York, NY 10014.

MAD LIBS® is fun to play with friends, but you can also play it by yourself! To begin with, DO NOT look at the story on the page below. Fill in the blanks on this page with the words called for. Then, using the words you have selected, fill in the blank spaces in the story.

Now you've created your own hilarious MAD LIBS® game!

INTERVIEW WITH A CELEBRITY VAMPIRE

FIRST NAME _____

NOUN _____

PERSON IN ROOM (MALE) _____

ADJECTIVE _____

NOUN _____

NOUN _____

PERSON IN ROOM _____

ADJECTIVE _____

ADVERB _____

ADJECTIVE _____

CELEBRITY (MALE) _____

ADJECTIVE _____

ADJECTIVE _____

CELEBRITY (FEMALE) _____

NOUN _____

MAD LIBS
INTERVIEW WITH A
CELEBRITY VAMPIRE

Recently I, _____ Walters, sat down with _____-
           FIRST NAME   NOUN

famous actor and vampire, _____, to discuss his
                                  PERSON IN ROOM (MALE)

most recent work, his run-in with the law, and how he met his

_____ fiancée.
   ADJECTIVE

Q: How does it feel to have recently won the Motion Picture

Academy _____ for your performance in the coming-
               NOUN

of-_____ movie, "The _____ Story"?
      NOUN   PERSON IN ROOM

A: It was a/an _____ honor just to be nominated.
                ADJECTIVE

Q: Last month you were _____ arrested by the
                           ADVERB

Hollywood police for allegedly trying to turn someone into a/an

_____ vampire. Can you comment on that?
   ADJECTIVE

A: My friend _____ *wanted* to become a vampire. It was
             CELEBRITY (MALE)

all a/an _____ misunderstanding.
      ADJECTIVE

Q: Tell us about your romance with the _____ actress,
                                ADJECTIVE

_____.
  CELEBRITY (FEMALE)

A: Let's just say I like to keep my private _____ private.
                                   NOUN

MAD LIBS® is fun to play with friends, but you can also play it by yourself! To begin with, DO NOT look at the story on the page below. Fill in the blanks on this page with the words called for. Then, using the words you have selected, fill in the blank spaces in the story.

Now you've created your own hilarious MAD LIBS® game!

A GRAVEYARD BASH

PERSON IN ROOM (MALE) _____

ADVERB _____

NOUN _____

ADJECTIVE _____

ADJECTIVE _____

VERB ENDING IN "ING" _____

NOUN _____

PLURAL NOUN _____

NOUN _____

ADJECTIVE _____

PERSON IN ROOM _____

SAME PERSON IN ROOM _____

MAD LIBS

A GRAVEYARD BASH

Dear _____,
PERSON IN ROOM (MALE)

You are _____ invited to the most ghoulish
ADVERB

_____ of the year!
NOUN

Where: The _____ cemetery on Eternity Lane
ADJECTIVE

When: Halloween night—at the _____ stroke of midnight
ADJECTIVE

Why: If you're undead and enjoy _____ until
VERB ENDING IN "ING"

    the break of _____, this shindig is for you! DJ
NOUN

    Afterlife will be spinning _____ all night, the
PLURAL NOUN

    Ghost of _____ Past will be bartending, and
NOUN

    the devil himself may even make a/an _____
ADJECTIVE

    guest appearance.

RSVP: Contact _____ the Zombie at _____-
PERSON IN ROOM   SAME PERSON IN ROOM

    zombie@zombiefriends.com.

From UNDEAD MAD LIBS® · Copyright © 2011 by Price Stern Sloan,
an imprint of Penguin Group (USA) Inc., 345 Hudson Street, New York, NY 10014.

MAD LIBS® is fun to play with friends, but you can also play it by yourself! To begin with, DO NOT look at the story on the page below. Fill in the blanks on this page with the words called for. Then, using the words you have selected, fill in the blank spaces in the story.

Now you've created your own hilarious MAD LIBS® game!

ARE YOU A VAMPIRE?

VERB _____

PART OF THE BODY _____

NOUN _____

ADJECTIVE _____

NOUN _____

NOUN _____

PLURAL NOUN _____

ADJECTIVE _____

ADVERB _____

ADJECTIVE _____

PLURAL NOUN _____

ADJECTIVE _____

MAD LIBS®

ARE YOU A VAMPIRE?

- Do you _____ with joy at the sight of blood?

VERB

- When you're hungry, does your _____ grow fangs?

PART OF THE BODY

- Do you sleep in a wooden _____ every day?

NOUN

- Do you avoid _____ sunlight for fear of turning into

ADJECTIVE

  a/an _____?

NOUN

- When you look into a/an _____, is your reflection missing?

NOUN

- Is biting _____ one of your _____

PLURAL NOUN ADJECTIVE

  nighttime activities?

- Have you ever _____ turned one of your _____

ADVERB ADJECTIVE

  friends into a vampire?

- Do you stay the same age no matter how many _____

PLURAL NOUN

  you've lived?

If you answered *yes* to any of these questions, you are probably

a/an _____ vampire.

ADJECTIVE

From UNDEAD MAD LIBS® · Copyright © 2011 by Price Stern Sloan,
an imprint of Penguin Group (USA) Inc., 345 Hudson Street, New York, NY 10014.

MAD LIBS® is fun to play with friends, but you can also play it by yourself! To begin with, DO NOT look at the story on the page below. Fill in the blanks on this page with the words called for. Then, using the words you have selected, fill in the blank spaces in the story.

Now you've created your own hilarious MAD LIBS® game!

DAWN OF THE UNDEAD

NOUN _____

ADJECTIVE _____

A PLACE _____

PLURAL NOUN _____

ADJECTIVE _____

PLURAL NOUN _____

ADJECTIVE _____

ADJECTIVE _____

NUMBER _____

PLURAL NOUN _____

ADJECTIVE _____

PART OF THE BODY (PLURAL) _____

VERB ENDING IN "ING" _____

NOUN _____

PLURAL NOUN _____

ADJECTIVE _____

MAD LIBS

DAWN OF THE UNDEAD

We interrupt your regularly scheduled _____ to bring
NOUN

you some _____ breaking news: A zombie outbreak in
ADJECTIVE

(the) _____ is causing mass hysteria among the city's
A PLACE

_____. The _____ zombie attack, believed
PLURAL NOUN   ADJECTIVE

to have started early this morning, has claimed a growing number of

_____. If you have any _____ information
PLURAL NOUN   ADJECTIVE

on the whereabouts of these _____ creatures, call your
ADJECTIVE

local police at 9-1-_____. Be on the lookout for anyone
NUMBER

with yellow _____ and a/an _____ look in
PLURAL NOUN   ADJECTIVE

his or her _____. Please note that these creatures
PART OF THE BODY (PLURAL)

make _____ sounds and walk in a trancelike
VERB ENDING IN "ING"

_____ when looking for _____ to feed on.
NOUN   PLURAL NOUN

Citizens are encouraged to stay indoors and remain calm, cool, and

_____.
ADJECTIVE

MAD LIBS® is fun to play with friends, but you can also play it by yourself! To begin with, DO NOT look at the story on the page below. Fill in the blanks on this page with the words called for. Then, using the words you have selected, fill in the blank spaces in the story.

Now you've created your own hilarious MAD LIBS® game!

HOW TO PERFORM A SÉANCE

ADJECTIVE _____

NOUN _____

ADJECTIVE _____

ADJECTIVE _____

PLURAL NOUN _____

NOUN _____

ADJECTIVE _____

ADJECTIVE _____

PLURAL NOUN _____

PLURAL NOUN _____

PART OF THE BODY (PLURAL) _____

NOUN _____

ADVERB _____

ADJECTIVE _____

MAD LIBS®
HOW TO PERFORM
A SÉANCE

Do you want a home, _____, home and not a haunted
                          ADJECTIVE

_____? Gather some _____ friends together
          NOUN   ADJECTIVE

late at night and have a/an _____ séance to get rid
                                  ADJECTIVE

of any evil spirits or ghostly _____ who just can't
                                    PLURAL NOUN

seem to cross over. First you'll need a wise _____ to
                                                    NOUN

preside over the gathering. He or she should have experience

talking to _____ spirits. Second, make sure to invite
               ADJECTIVE

friends who feel really _____ about being there. No
                              ADJECTIVE

scaredy-_____ allowed. Once your friends arrive, light
          PLURAL NOUN

some _____ to set the mood, sit next to one another,
          PLURAL NOUN

and hold _____. Then the medium should say, "Dear
          PART OF THE BODY (PLURAL)

Spirit, if you can hear us, tap three times on the _____."
                                                          NOUN

If all goes _____, your _____ house will be
                ADVERB   ADJECTIVE

ghost-free in no time.

MAD LIBS® is fun to play with friends, but you can also play it by yourself! To begin with, DO NOT look at the story on the page below. Fill in the blanks on this page with the words called for. Then, using the words you have selected, fill in the blank spaces in the story.

Now you've created your own hilarious MAD LIBS® game!

DEMON DOS AND DON'TS

ADJECTIVE _____

PERSON IN ROOM _____

ADJECTIVE _____

PLURAL NOUN _____

PART OF THE BODY _____

PLURAL NOUN _____

PERSON IN ROOM _____

PLURAL NOUN _____

NOUN _____

PART OF THE BODY (PLURAL) _____

ADJECTIVE _____

PLURAL NOUN _____

MAD LIBS®

DEMON DOS AND DON'TS

When you come across a demon—the _____ spawn
                                        ADJECTIVE

of _____—beware. These supernatural, super-
      PERSON IN ROOM

_____ _____ are pure evil, so take heed of
   ADJECTIVE   PLURAL NOUN

these dos and don'ts.

Do stay away from pitchfork-holding, fanged-_____
                                                  PART OF THE BODY

creatures.

Don't befriend, steal from, or give _____ to a demon.
                                          PLURAL NOUN

Do be wary of anyone named Balthazar, Diablo, or Overlord

_____.
   PERSON IN ROOM

Don't accept any contracts from a demon promising millions of

_____ for signing your _____ away.
   PLURAL NOUN   NOUN

Do check your friends' _____. Do they have red
                            PART OF THE BODY (PLURAL)

horns? If so, run! Those aren't your _____ friends, those
                                        ADJECTIVE

are your worst _____!
                  PLURAL NOUN

MAD LIBS® is fun to play with friends, but you can also play it by yourself! To begin with, DO NOT look at the story on the page below. Fill in the blanks on this page with the words called for. Then, using the words you have selected, fill in the blank spaces in the story.

Now you've created your own hilarious MAD LIBS® game!

A NIGHT AT THE UNDEAD HOSPITAL

PERSON IN ROOM (FEMALE) _____

OCCUPATION _____

CELEBRITY _____

ADJECTIVE _____

NOUN _____

ADJECTIVE _____

ADJECTIVE _____

ADJECTIVE _____

PART OF THE BODY (PLURAL) _____

PLURAL NOUN _____

NOUN _____

ADJECTIVE _____

ADJECTIVE _____

PART OF THE BODY _____

LAST NAME _____

ADJECTIVE _____

NOUN _____

MAD LIBS®
A NIGHT AT THE
UNDEAD HOSPITAL

_____ just finished her first night as a/an
PERSON IN ROOM (FEMALE)

_____ at Saint _____'s Hospital for the
OCCUPATION   CELEBRITY

Undead. At first, she was excited about her _____ job.
                                                ADJECTIVE

She thought of it as a charity _____, healing such
                                    NOUN

_____ creatures as zombies and vampires when no
ADJECTIVE

one else would. But now she's not sure she'll ever go back. The

halls were dark and _____. Everywhere she turned,
                        ADJECTIVE

she felt patients staring at her with a/an _____ look
                                              ADJECTIVE

in their _____. She had to put casts on skeletons
PART OF THE BODY (PLURAL)

with broken _____, give _____ injections
              PLURAL NOUN   NOUN

to blood-_____ vampires, and heal _____
          ADJECTIVE   ADJECTIVE

zombies while they foamed at the _____. Dr.
                                    PART OF THE BODY

_____ even asked her if she'd like to become a vampire
LAST NAME

with him! The experience was truly _____. And worst
                                        ADJECTIVE

of all she now has two _____ marks on her neck that
                          NOUN

won't go away!

From UNDEAD MAD LIBS® · Copyright © 2011 by Price Stern Sloan,
an imprint of Penguin Group (USA) Inc., 345 Hudson Street, New York, NY 10014.

MAD LIBS® is fun to play with friends, but you can also play it by yourself! To begin with, DO NOT look at the story on the page below. Fill in the blanks on this page with the words called for. Then, using the words you have selected, fill in the blank spaces in the story.

Now you've created your own hilarious MAD LIBS® game!

BLENDING IN ON HALLOWEEN NIGHT

NOUN _____

ADVERB _____

ADJECTIVE _____

ADJECTIVE _____

NOUN _____

NOUN _____

ADJECTIVE _____

NOUN _____

ADJECTIVE _____

PLURAL NOUN _____

NOUN _____

ADJECTIVE _____

ADJECTIVE _____

NOUN _____

MAD LIBS
BLENDING IN ON
HALLOWEEN NIGHT

If you're a ghoul, a zombie, or a/an _____, Halloween is
NOUN

the one night a year when you can walk among the living. In order

to blend in _____, follow these tried-and-_____
ADVERB   ADJECTIVE

tips for passing as a human.

• Be yourself! Who needs a costume when you're as _____
ADJECTIVE

as you are? Besides, no one wants to see a zombie dressed like

Little Bo _____ or Super-_____.
NOUN   NOUN

• If someone offers you _____ candy, do not be
ADJECTIVE

alarmed. Act natural and say "Trick or _____!"
NOUN

• Remember: You're trying to blend in. This means you can't bite

anyone. But you *can* scare people! What's Halloween without a

few _____ shrieks?
ADJECTIVE

• Lastly, have fun! Go to human parties and bob for _____,
PLURAL NOUN

carve a/an _____, or enter a contest for the most
NOUN

_____ costume. With your _____ looks, you just
ADJECTIVE   ADJECTIVE

might win first _____!
NOUN

From UNDEAD MAD LIBS® · Copyright © 2011 by Price Stern Sloan,
an imprint of Penguin Group (USA) Inc., 345 Hudson Street, New York, NY 10014.

MAD LIBS® is fun to play with friends, but you can also play it by yourself! To begin with, DO NOT look at the story on the page below. Fill in the blanks on this page with the words called for. Then, using the words you have selected, fill in the blank spaces in the story.

Now you've created your own hilarious MAD LIBS® game!

THE STORY OF VAMPIRE CAT

ADJECTIVE _____

ADJECTIVE _____

ADJECTIVE _____

PART OF THE BODY _____

ADJECTIVE _____

ADJECTIVE _____

PERSON IN ROOM (MALE) _____

NOUN _____

ADVERB _____

ADJECTIVE _____

PLURAL NOUN _____

ADJECTIVE _____

NUMBER _____

SILLY WORD _____

VERB ENDING IN "ING" _____

PLURAL NOUN_____

ADJECTIVE _____

ADJECTIVE _____

MAD LIBS
THE STORY OF VAMPIRE CAT

Once upon a time, a vampire was desperate for some _____
_____ADJECTIVE

blood. There were no humans around, and he was on the verge

of a/an _____ breakdown. He was searching everywhere for
_____ADJECTIVE

victims when he spotted a/an _____ tabby cat that made his
_____ADJECTIVE

_____ water. He decided to make this _____
PART OF THE BODY _____ADJECTIVE

little furball his student as well as his _____ victim. The
_____ADJECTIVE

cat, renamed Count _____ VonCat, became the
_____PERSON IN ROOM (MALE)

world's first feline vampire. Count VonCat terrorized the town of

_____-ville and used his _____ sweet purr
NOUN _____ADVERB

and _____ stare to lure innocent _____
_____ADJECTIVE PLURAL NOUN

into his clutches. To this day, Count VonCat continues his hunt—

even at the ripe _____ age of _____.
_____ADJECTIVE NUMBER

He was last seen in the quiet village of _____,
_____SILLY WORD

_____ in alleyways and preying on _____
VERB ENDING IN "ING" PLURAL NOUN

who fall for his _____ cuteness and _____ charm.
_____ADJECTIVE _____ADJECTIVE

MAD LIBS® is fun to play with friends, but you can also play it by yourself! To begin with, DO NOT look at the story on the page below. Fill in the blanks on this page with the words called for. Then, using the words you have selected, fill in the blank spaces in the story.

Now you've created your own hilarious MAD LIBS® game!

THE CASE OF THE LIVING SKELETON

VERB ENDING IN "ING" _____

ADJECTIVE _____

ADJECTIVE _____

PLURAL NOUN _____

PERSON IN ROOM (MALE) _____

NOUN _____

ADJECTIVE _____

ADJECTIVE _____

NOUN _____

ADVERB _____

PART OF THE BODY _____

NOUN _____

ADJECTIVE _____

NOUN _____

MAD LIBS®
THE CASE OF THE LIVING SKELETON

It hasn't yet been proven, but I'm fairly certain that the skeleton

in the biology classroom is alive and _____. There's a

VERB ENDING IN "ING"

rumor that the _____ thing comes to life after school,

ADJECTIVE

performing _____ experiments on frogs and dissecting

ADJECTIVE

_____. And _____ swears that when he

PLURAL NOUN   PERSON IN ROOM (MALE)

walked past the classroom after _____ practice, he saw

NOUN

the skeleton dancing. Finally I worked up the _____

ADJECTIVE

courage to solve this _____ mystery. One day, I hid

ADJECTIVE

underneath a/an _____ and waited for the biology

NOUN

teacher to leave. Then I walked _____ toward the

ADVERB

skeleton, tapped him on the shoulder, and bravely said, "Hello?"

The skeleton turned, slowly raising his right _____

PART OF THE BODY

to wave at me! I ran out of that room faster than a speeding

_____. Now I have a/an _____ excuse for

NOUN   ADJECTIVE

never attending biology _____ again!

NOUN

MAD LIBS® is fun to play with friends, but you can also play it by yourself! To begin with, DO NOT look at the story on the page below. Fill in the blanks on this page with the words called for. Then, using the words you have selected, fill in the blank spaces in the story.

Now you've created your own hilarious MAD LIBS® game!

HOW TO WARD OFF A VAMPIRE

PLURAL NOUN _____

NOUN _____

ADJECTIVE _____

NOUN _____

ADJECTIVE _____

ADJECTIVE _____

ADJECTIVE _____

VERB _____

PLURAL NOUN _____

PLURAL NOUN _____

NOUN _____

PART OF THE BODY (PLURAL) _____

NOUN _____

NOUN _____

ADVERB _____

PART OF THE BODY _____

MAD LIBS®
HOW TO WARD
OFF A VAMPIRE

All _____ beware. Fending off vampires takes more than
    PLURAL NOUN

common _____ and _____ intuition. Sure, you
      NOUN   ADJECTIVE

could carry around a sharp, wooden _____ to stop an attack,
                         NOUN

but you should also follow these four _____ suggestions:
                       ADJECTIVE

1. Vampires love the dark and hate the _____ sun, so
                       ADJECTIVE

   run your _____ errands in the daytime and don't
            ADJECTIVE

   _____ alone in the middle of the night.
     VERB

2. Vampires despise garlic and are allergic to holy _____,
                       PLURAL NOUN

   so carry these _____ on your _____ at all times.
           PLURAL NOUN   NOUN

3. Vampires absolutely can't stand the sight of their hideous

   _____ in a mirror. So always have a handheld
   PART OF THE BODY (PLURAL)

   _____ in your pocket.
   NOUN

4. If you really want that pesky vampire to bite the dust and

   cross over to the other _____, legend has it that
                    NOUN

   there is only one way to _____ stop a vampire:
                    ADVERB

   Cut off its _____.
        PART OF THE BODY

MAD LIBS® is fun to play with friends, but you can also play it by yourself! To begin with, DO NOT look at the story on the page below. Fill in the blanks on this page with the words called for. Then, using the words you have selected, fill in the blank spaces in the story.

Now you've created your own hilarious MAD LIBS® game!

FACTS ABOUT GHOULS

ADJECTIVE _____

ADVERB _____

NOUN _____

PLURAL NOUN _____

ADJECTIVE _____

ADJECTIVE _____

PLURAL NOUN _____

ADJECTIVE _____

PLURAL NOUN _____

PART OF THE BODY (PLURAL) _____

ADJECTIVE _____

ADJECTIVE _____

PLURAL NOUN _____

MAD LIBS

FACTS ABOUT GHOULS

Of all the undead creatures, _____ ghouls are probably
ADJECTIVE

the most misunderstood. Contrary to popular belief, ghouls are

_____ different from ghosts. They are undead monsters
ADVERB

who live in _____-yards and survive by gnawing
NOUN

on the _____ found in _____ graves. The
PLURAL NOUN   ADJECTIVE

_____ appearance of these evil _____ may
ADJECTIVE   PLURAL NOUN

shock you. Ghouls are extremely thin and _____ with
ADJECTIVE

sharp teeth and _____, and their _____
PLURAL NOUN   PART OF THE BODY (PLURAL)

are wrinkled and _____. Ghouls sleep underground
ADJECTIVE

and emerge in packs at night—so next time you're wandering in

a/an _____ cemetery after dusk, be careful. These
ADJECTIVE

fiendish _____ might mistake you for dinner!
PLURAL NOUN

MAD LIBS® is fun to play with friends, but you can also play it by yourself! To begin with, DO NOT look at the story on the page below. Fill in the blanks on this page with the words called for. Then, using the words you have selected, fill in the blank spaces in the story.

Now you've created your own hilarious MAD LIBS® game!

A DIFFERENT KIND OF MOTHER

ADJECTIVE _____

PERSON IN ROOM (FEMALE) _____

ADJECTIVE _____

PLURAL NOUN _____

NOUN _____

PART OF THE BODY (PLURAL) _____

ADVERB _____

NOUN _____

ADJECTIVE _____

PART OF THE BODY _____

ADJECTIVE _____

PLURAL NOUN _____

PLURAL NOUN _____

LAST NAME _____

ADVERB _____

ADJECTIVE _____

PART OF THE BODY _____

NOUN _____

COLOR _____

MAD LIBS®
A DIFFERENT KIND
OF MOTHER

Yesterday after school I went to my _____ friend
                                          ADJECTIVE

_____'s home to meet her _____
PERSON IN ROOM (FEMALE)   ADJECTIVE

family. On the way there, she warned me about her mother: "My

mom's not like other _____. She's . . . different." "No big
                          PLURAL NOUN

_____," I said, shrugging my _____. As
NOUN   PART OF THE BODY (PLURAL)

we approached the house, the door swung open _____.
                                                      ADVERB

One look and I jumped at least a/an _____ high. My
                                          NOUN

friend's mother was a/an _____ mummy, wrapped
                              ADJECTIVE

head to _____ in _____ strips of white
          PART OF THE BODY   ADJECTIVE

_____! I was literally shaking in my _____.
PLURAL NOUN   PLURAL NOUN

"Hi, I'm Ms. _____, the mummy mommy. You're just
                  LAST NAME

in time," she said. "For what?" I asked _____. "Dinner!
                                              ADVERB

And I've got a/an _____ surprise: We're having my
                      ADJECTIVE

famous _____ lasagna." I didn't have to say a/an
          PART OF THE BODY

_____. I turned as _____ as a sheet and
NOUN   COLOR

headed straight for home.

From UNDEAD MAD LIBS® · Copyright © 2011 by Price Stern Sloan,
an imprint of Penguin Group (USA) Inc., 345 Hudson Street, New York, NY 10014.

MAD LIBS® is fun to play with friends, but you can also play it by yourself! To begin with, DO NOT look at the story on the page below. Fill in the blanks on this page with the words called for. Then, using the words you have selected, fill in the blank spaces in the story.

Now you've created your own hilarious MAD LIBS® game!

DRACULA

FIRST NAME _____

NOUN _____

ADJECTIVE _____

ADJECTIVE _____

NOUN _____

FIRST NAME (MALE) _____

PLURAL NOUN _____

PLURAL NOUN _____

PLURAL NOUN _____

VERB ENDING IN "ING" _____

CELEBRITY (FEMALE) _____

NOUN _____

ADJECTIVE _____

NOUN _____

ADVERB _____

DRACULA

_____ Stoker's *Dracula* is a famous _____,
<u>FIRST NAME</u>   <u>NOUN</u>

written in 1897, that tells the _____ story of Count
                                                <u>ADJECTIVE</u>

Dracula, a vampire living in a/an _____ castle. The story
                                                        <u>ADJECTIVE</u>

begins with a young _____, _____ Harker,
                                        <u>NOUN</u>   <u>FIRST NAME (MALE)</u>

who visits the Count in order to discuss estate plans and other

legal _____. Harker quickly learns that Count Dracula is
            <u>PLURAL NOUN</u>

one of the most dangerous _____ of all time. The Count
                                            <u>PLURAL NOUN</u>

puts Harker under a spell that makes him fall in love with three

of Dracula's _____. Then the blood-_____
                    <u>PLURAL NOUN</u>   <u>VERB ENDING IN "ING"</u>

Dracula takes a woman named _____ as his victim.
                                                <u>CELEBRITY (FEMALE)</u>

Thankfully, by the book's end, Dracula is killed and turned into

_____ dust. The _____ Harker gets married to
          <u>NOUN</u>   <u>ADJECTIVE</u>

a beautiful _____ and lives _____ ever after.
                    <u>NOUN</u>   <u>ADVERB</u>

MAD LIBS® is fun to play with friends, but you can also play it by yourself! To begin with, DO NOT look at the story on the page below. Fill in the blanks on this page with the words called for. Then, using the words you have selected, fill in the blank spaces in the story.

Now you've created your own hilarious MAD LIBS® game!

TEST YOUR UNDEAD IQ

ADJECTIVE _____

PLURAL NOUN _____

NOUN _____

ADJECTIVE _____

NOUN _____

PLURAL NOUN _____

NOUN _____

NOUN _____

NOUN _____

ADJECTIVE _____

NOUN _____

PERSON IN ROOM _____

NOUN _____

ADJECTIVE _____

ADJECTIVE _____

NOUN _____

ADJECTIVE _____

MAD LIBS

TEST YOUR UNDEAD IQ

Are you an undead expert? Take this _____ quiz to find out!
                                   ADJECTIVE

1. Where do vampires sleep? a) with the fishes, b) on the

   beach so they can catch some _____, c) inside a/an
                                  PLURAL NOUN

   _____, or d) in a/an _____ coffin
        NOUN   ADJECTIVE

2. What is a zombie's favorite snack? a) _____ salad,
                                              NOUN

   b) chocolate-covered _____, c) _____
                          PLURAL NOUN   NOUN

   bits, or d) brains

3. Where do ghouls go to meet ghoul friends? a) the grocery

   _____, b) the _____ park, c) a/an
        NOUN   NOUN

   _____ school, or d) the grave-_____
      ADJECTIVE   NOUN

4. How do mummies become undead? a) they ask _____
                                               PERSON IN ROOM

   nicely, b) they travel through time using a/an _____
                                                      NOUN

   machine, c) they earn extra _____ grades in school, or
                                 ADJECTIVE

   d) they get cursed by a/an _____ sorcerer
                                ADJECTIVE

If you answered mostly Ds, you're a real undead _____!
                                                     NOUN

Your _____ expertise will come in handy—in this life
        ADJECTIVE

and beyond . . .

From UNDEAD MAD LIBS® · Copyright © 2011 by Price Stern Sloan,
a division of Penguin Young Readers Group, 345 Hudson Street, New York, NY 10014.

MAD LIBS® is fun to play with friends, but you can also play it by yourself! To begin with, DO NOT look at the story on the page below. Fill in the blanks on this page with the words called for. Then, using the words you have selected, fill in the blank spaces in the story.

Now you've created your own hilarious MAD LIBS® game!

ANYTHING YOU VOODOO, I VOODOO BETTER

PERSON IN ROOM (MALE) _____

ADVERB _____

NUMBER _____

NOUN _____

NOUN _____

A PLACE _____

NOUN _____

VERB _____

NOUN _____

ADJECTIVE _____

NOUN _____

ADJECTIVE _____

ADJECTIVE _____

PLURAL NOUN _____

ADJECTIVE _____

MAD LIBS

ANYTHING YOU VOODOO, I VOODOO BETTER

My name is Sorcerer _____, and I am
                        PERSON IN ROOM (MALE)

a/an _____ trained voodoo master. In my years as a
            ADVERB

sorcerer, I have cursed more than _____ dead people
                                        NUMBER

and turned them into _____-eating zombies. And now
                            NOUN

that they're under my _____ for eternity, I can take
                            NOUN

over (the) _____! Many will join me in my quest for
                A PLACE

_____ domination. All I have to do is hold a séance, tell
        NOUN

everyone to _____ into my crystal _____,
                    VERB   NOUN

think _____ thoughts, and stay very, very still. Then I
            ADJECTIVE

use a special _____ to turn them into crusty, creepy,
                    NOUN

_____ zombies. From that point on, I can use mind
        ADJECTIVE

control to make them attack _____ cities and eat
                                    ADJECTIVE

unsuspecting _____. I'm so powerful you might be
                PLURAL NOUN

under my _____ spell already . . .
                ADJECTIVE

MAD LIBS® is fun to play with friends, but you can also play it by yourself! To begin with, DO NOT look at the story on the page below. Fill in the blanks on this page with the words called for. Then, using the words you have selected, fill in the blank spaces in the story.

Now you've created your own hilarious MAD LIBS® game!

FACTS ABOUT MUMMIES

ADJECTIVE _____

ADJECTIVE _____

PLURAL NOUN _____

PART OF THE BODY _____

PLURAL NOUN _____

PERSON IN ROOM (MALE) _____

A PLACE _____

PLURAL NOUN _____

PART OF THE BODY _____

A PLACE _____

ADJECTIVE _____

ADJECTIVE _____

ADJECTIVE _____

NOUN _____

NOUN _____

MAD LIBS

FACTS ABOUT MUMMIES

The history of the mummy goes all the way back to _____
ADJECTIVE

Egypt, where mummification was a way of honoring the

_____ dead. Ancient Egyptians wrapped the bodies of
ADJECTIVE

important _____ from head to _____ to
PLURAL NOUN   PART OF THE BODY

preserve them for eternity. Then they put them in a tomb along with

their most important _____ to carry them into the afterlife.
PLURAL NOUN

Perhaps the most famous mummy is King _____, who
PERSON IN ROOM (MALE)

is currently on display at (the) _____. But one of the
A PLACE

oldest _____ ever found is the Andean mummified
PLURAL NOUN

_____, which is six thousand years old and from
PART OF THE BODY

(the) _____. While mummification is no longer in
A PLACE

_____ fashion, some say that if a mummy's _____
ADJECTIVE   ADJECTIVE

tomb is disturbed, the _____ person inside will rise from
ADJECTIVE

the _____ and haunt the intruder for the rest of his or
NOUN

her _____.
NOUN

MAD LIBS® is fun to play with friends, but you can also play it by yourself! To begin with, DO NOT look at the story on the page below. Fill in the blanks on this page with the words called for. Then, using the words you have selected, fill in the blank spaces in the story.

Now you've created your own hilarious MAD LIBS® game!

UNDEAD CLASSIFIED ADS

ADJECTIVE _____

PLURAL NOUN _____

NOUN _____

ADJECTIVE _____

NOUN _____

NUMBER _____

ADJECTIVE _____

A PLACE _____

PERSON IN ROOM (MALE) _____

ADJECTIVE _____

ADJECTIVE _____

PLURAL NOUN _____

PART OF THE BODY _____

NOUN _____

ADJECTIVE _____

MAD LIBS

UNDEAD CLASSIFIED ADS

Are you a/an _____ vampire, zombie, mummy, or
                    ADJECTIVE

ghoul in need of that special something? Look no further than

the *New Undead Times* classified ads, where you'll find all the

_____ your evil heart desires.
PLURAL NOUN

Skeleton Seeks Single, Bony _____: Male skeleton
                                          NOUN

seeking a/an _____, easygoing, and _____-loving
              ADJECTIVE   NOUN

lady skeleton to wine and dine. Must have all _____
                                                    NUMBER

bones intact. Those with _____ personalities preferred.
                              ADJECTIVE

Coffin for Sale! Perfect condition. Used for only two centuries.

Great for a bedroom, basement, or (the) _____. Contact
                                          A PLACE

Count _____ for details. _____ inquiries only.
        PERSON IN ROOM (MALE)   ADJECTIVE

Zombie Puppies for Adoption: These _____, little
                                              ADJECTIVE

creatures might tear up your favorite pair of _____,
                                                  PLURAL NOUN

foam at the _____, or try to turn you into a/an
                PART OF THE BODY

_____, but who cares! They're just too _____
        NOUN   ADJECTIVE

to pass up.

MAD LIBS® is fun to play with friends, but you can also play it by yourself! To begin with, DO NOT look at the story on the page below. Fill in the blanks on this page with the words called for. Then, using the words you have selected, fill in the blank spaces in the story.

Now you've created your own hilarious MAD LIBS® game!

HOW TO SURVIVE A ZOMBIE ATTACK

NOUN _____

NOUN _____

ADJECTIVE _____

ADJECTIVE _____

PART OF THE BODY _____

NOUN _____

ADJECTIVE _____

PLURAL NOUN _____

NOUN _____

ADJECTIVE _____

NOUN _____

ADJECTIVE _____

PLURAL NOUN _____

PLURAL NOUN _____

HOW TO SURVIVE
A ZOMBIE ATTACK

Are zombies trying to take over your _____? Grab
                                          NOUN

a/an _____ immediately and start fending off those
          NOUN

_____ monsters before you become one yourself! Here
   ADJECTIVE

are some _____ tips for survival.
              ADJECTIVE

• Zombies want to eat your _____, so put on a/an
                              PART OF THE BODY

  _____ before heading out to save your _____ town.
      NOUN   ADJECTIVE

• You can become a zombie via a zombie bite. Therefore, wear a suit

  made of _____ to protect your skin. If you see that one of
            PLURAL NOUN

  your friends has a bite, stay far away. That friend may now be a/an

  _____!
      NOUN

• Don't waste your _____ time trying to turn someone
                        ADJECTIVE

  you know back into a/an _____. There's no way to
                              NOUN

  un-zombie a/an _____ zombie.
                      ADJECTIVE

• The phrase "Keep your friends close and your _____
                                                    PLURAL NOUN

  closer" does not apply here! If you spot any zombies, run for the

  _____.
      PLURAL NOUN